| Adapted by | Illustrated by | Designed by |
| --- | --- | --- |
| **Josh Crute** | **Matt Kaufenberg** | **Tony Fejeran** |

 **A GOLDEN BOOK • NEW YORK**

rhcbooks.com

ISBN 978-0-7364-3978-7 (trade) — ISBN 978-0-7364-3979-4 (ebook)

Printed in the United States of America

10 9 8 7 6 5 4 3

**H**owdy, partner! Meet **Woody**, the sheriff round these parts. Woody loved his kid, Andy, and was the leader of the toys in Andy's room. But sometimes he needed help. Thankfully, his best friend, **Bo Peep**, was always there to lend a hand.

Then one day, **everything changed**.

Bo Peep was getting a new kid—and
Woody was **staying behind**.

Years later, Woody got a new kid, too. Her name was **Bonnie**. At **kindergarten orientation**, she was a little nervous.

Luckily, she had a sheriff around! When
a boy took her art supplies, Woody rustled
them up, along with some new ones. Bonnie
used her **imagination** to put them together
to make a new friend. . . .

**Forky!**

To Woody's surprise, Forky **came to life—**
just like the other toys!

Forky was surprised, too. He didn't
think he was a toy at all—he was a spork!
So when Bonnie's family went on a road
trip in their RV . . .

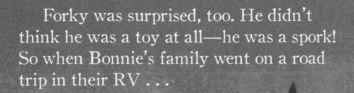

**Forky
made a
break
for it!**

Sheriff Woody would never leave
anyone behind. He jumped out the
window after Forky.

Woody took Forky to the next town to catch up with Bonnie. Then something in the window of an antiques store caught his eye . . . **Bo's lamp!**

Woody and Forky went into the store. Instead of finding Bo, they saw a doll named **Gabby Gabby**. She seemed friendly at first—but then she said she wanted Woody's voice box. She told her team to capture Woody and Forky!

Woody escaped to a nearby playground, where he saw a familiar face—**Bo Peep!** She and her tiny friend, **Giggle McDimples**, were traveling with a group of toys to find kids to play with. Bo said she would help Woody rescue Forky!

Meanwhile, **Buzz Lightyear** was searching for Woody and Forky. The brave space ranger followed their trail to a carnival, but he got stuck to a prize wall. He met a couple of toys, **Ducky and Bunny**. Buzz accidentally set both of them free!

Buzz found Woody and Bo, and the whole group sneaked into the antiques store. Forky was trapped in a **tall cabinet**.

The store's cat, **Dragon**, roamed the aisles, looking for stray toys to gobble up. The friends had to figure out a plan.

Bo found **Duke Caboom**, Canada's greatest stuntman. He would help rescue Forky, as well as Bo's sheep. They had been captured, too.

Duke leaped across the aisle to the cabinet. **But he didn't make it.** Dragon spotted him and the toys!

Bo found her sheep just as Dragon began to **chase** Duke. The toys held on tight!

They made it out of the store—but
Forky was still inside. Most of the group
was too **tired and scared** to try a new
plan. They decided to leave.

But Woody needed to get Forky. He made a
deal with Gabby Gabby. In exchange for Forky,
he gave her his **voice box**. And he would take her
to Bonnie so she could have a kid, too.

The toys returned to help Woody and Gabby Gabby. But there was only **one way** to reach Bonnie. They went to the carnival and rode to the top of the Ferris wheel. Then they tied a long string around Duke's bike.

Duke took a deep breath, **revved his engine** . . .

. . . and **SOARED** over the crowd!

Thanks to Duke, the toys zipped across the carnival on the string. Then Gabby Gabby noticed a girl who was lost and needed a friend. Gabby Gabby was perfect for her! The girl hugged the doll close just before she found her parents. **Gabby Gabby got a kid!**

The toys found Bonnie. She was **thrilled** to see Forky again!

Woody loved seeing the two of them **so happy**.

And he was glad to be **reunited** with his friends.

Woody realized that lost and lonely toys
were everywhere, and he wanted to help them.
He knew that with Bo and their friends, he could
**accomplish anything**!